The Hunt: Into the Frost

This is a work of fiction. Similarities to real people, places, or events are entirely coincidental.

THE HUNT: INTO THE FROST

First edition. September 22, 2024.

Copyright © 2024 Edward Heath.

ISBN: 979-8227686442

Written by Edward Heath.

To all my family, friends, and readers, I love you all

Prologue

"Welcome, everyone, to the newest season of *The Hunt*—where survival is the only way out! This year, we're taking you to the freezing, unforgiving wilderness of the Antarctic, where six brave contestants will face off against the elements, the hunters, and each other in a battle for their very lives!"

The announcer's voice booms across millions of screens, his tone electric with excitement. The camera pans across a massive digital screen behind him, displaying images of jagged ice cliffs, frozen tundra, and icy waters stretching to the horizon. It's an environment where danger lurks at every corner, and survival is a feat in itself.

"Now, this season brings an all-new twist—three of our contestants have criminal pasts, and three are completely innocent. But all of them have volunteered to face the ultimate challenge, knowing the stakes. One of them will claim victory and their freedom, but first, they must endure."

The show transitions to a series of interviews with the contestants, giving the audience a glimpse of their personalities, backgrounds, and why they've chosen to risk it all.

The camera zooms in on one of the contestants—a sharp-eyed man named Caleb. His expression is calm, but there's a hint of steel in his voice as he speaks.

"I'm here to prove something," Caleb says, his hands clasped in front of him. "My past doesn't define me. This is my chance to start over."

The screen cuts to another contestant, a woman named Sarah, her posture more defensive.

"I didn't do anything wrong," she says, her voice trembling slightly. "But if this is what it takes to get my life back, then I'll do it."

The interviews continue, showcasing the mixture of determination and fear in each contestant's face. Some are hardened by their pasts, while others seem out of place, their innocence clouding their decision to join the game.

As the interviews end, the camera returns to the announcer, who grins at the screen.

"Now, let's move on to the main event—the moment they lose everything. Our contestants are about to have their memories wiped, their minds reset as they enter the arctic wasteland. It's time for the chips to be implanted, and once they're dropped in the frozen wilderness, there will be no going back."

The screen shifts to show the contestants being led, one by one, into sterile rooms. Each is fitted with cold-weather gear and microchipped. Their eyes glaze over as the memories of their lives are erased, replaced only by a survival instinct and the drive to make it through the game.

With a flicker, the camera cuts to a wide shot of the Antarctic, a helicopter hovering above the ice. One by one, the contestants are dropped into the frozen wilderness, scattered across the snow and left with only their cold-weather gear and minimal supplies.

"Six contestants, one icy wasteland, and danger around every corner. Who will outlast the cold, the hunters, and each other? Let *The Hunt* begin!"

The screen fades to black as the show cuts to a commercial break, the excitement in the audience palpable.

Chapter 1: Awakening in the Ice

The cold was the first thing they felt—biting, relentless, and unforgiving.

Caleb's eyes fluttered open, his breath coming out in shallow, misty puffs as he blinked against the blinding white landscape around him. The sharp sting of frost bit into his exposed face, and for a moment, he could hardly move, his body sluggish from the cold. His fingers fumbled with the layers of his cold-weather gear, trying to gather enough warmth to keep himself from freezing.

Where am I?

The question rang through his mind, but there was no answer. He couldn't remember. He didn't know how he got here or why he felt so disoriented. All he knew was the ice, the snow, and the bone-chilling cold.

The heat pack nestled in his gloves had already started to lose its warmth, and a dull sense of panic began to settle in his chest. Shakily, he reached into one of his pockets and pulled out a fresh heat pack, tearing it open and shaking it vigorously until it began to warm up in his hands. It wasn't much, but it kept the cold at bay for the moment.

As he stood, scanning the white expanse, he noticed a small pack lying in the snow near him. He opened it quickly, finding a few essentials: more heat packs—12 in total—an emergency first aid kit, a couple of MRE rations, flint and steel, and two chemical glow sticks. His fingers were already stiff from the cold as he fumbled with the supplies, his breath coming in heavy puffs that dissipated in the icy air.

The cold-weather gear he wore was thick, designed to fight off frostbite, but it felt just barely enough. The layers of insulation insulated him from the wind, but the chill still seeped through, threatening to freeze him from the inside out.

He glanced around, his vision filled with nothing but snow and ice stretching endlessly in every direction. The wind howled like a distant scream, and as he took a few steps forward, something caught his eye—a shadow moving in the distance. He blinked, squinting against the glare of the sun reflecting off the ice. Was that…someone?

His heart skipped a beat, a mixture of hope and fear twisting in his gut. He wasn't alone out here. But were they friend or foe?

Not far away, Sarah stumbled through the snow, her hands trembling as she struggled to keep the heat packs pressed against her body. Her mind was a haze of confusion and fear. Like Caleb, she had no memory of who she was, why she was here, or what had happened to her before this moment. All she knew was that she had woken up in the middle of this frozen wasteland, with the overwhelming need to survive.

Her eyes scanned her surroundings, looking for any signs of shelter or warmth, but there was nothing. Just the endless stretch of ice and snow.

As she moved, her foot hit something solid beneath the snow. She knelt down, brushing the snow aside to reveal a pack similar to the one Caleb had found. Inside were the same essentials: heat packs, first aid kit, MREs, flint, steel, and glow sticks. She stuffed the items into her pockets, her hands moving quickly despite the cold.

But as she stood, a flicker of movement in the distance caught her attention. A figure—tall, cloaked in white, almost blending into the snowy landscape.

A chill ran down her spine, but it wasn't from the cold. Something about the figure felt off, dangerous even. Her instincts screamed at her to run, but her feet were frozen in place, fear gripping her tightly.

What is that?

The figure moved closer, and Sarah's breath hitched in her throat. Whoever—or whatever—it was, they weren't friendly. She didn't know how she knew, but every fiber of her being screamed danger.

Without thinking, she turned and ran, her feet slipping in the snow as she struggled to escape. The cold bit at her face, the wind whipping against her as she fled into the white void.

One by one, the others woke up, each in different parts of the arctic wasteland, disoriented and freezing. They, too, found their gear, barely enough to keep them alive, and each spotted the shadows lurking in the distance.

The hunters.

They moved silently, always at the edge of vision, watching, waiting. The survivors, unaware of the true nature of the game they were now part of, could only feel the looming presence of something dark and deadly.

There was no shelter in sight, no safety from the cold or the hunters. Only survival, as the endless snow stretched on and on.

Chapter 2: The Frozen Divide

The vast, white wasteland stretched endlessly in every direction, broken only by the occasional jagged ice cliff or frozen ridge. The cold was merciless, cutting through layers of clothing and seeping into the bones of those scattered across the terrain.

Jake, a cold-weather survivalist, crouched low as he examined the ice under his feet. He was built for this—broad-shouldered, rugged, his face weathered by years of surviving in extreme environments. His instincts kicked in, calculating the dangers of the terrain, the ice sheets, and the harsh wind that howled across the landscape. Every sound, every gust of wind carried with it a warning: stay alert, or you die.

Nearby, Harper trudged through the snow, the weight of her gear making every step a struggle. She hadn't said much since waking up, but her eyes darted around, taking in the sights and sounds. Slung over her back was a large cold-weather tent—an unexpected but welcome piece of equipment she had found in her pack. The tent could shelter up to ten people, but she wasn't sure if she'd be willing to share it with anyone yet. Survival, after all, wasn't a group activity.

Suddenly, the silence was shattered by the distant sound of a low growl. Jake's eyes narrowed as he glanced toward the horizon, where a hulking shape was moving through the snow—a polar bear, massive and menacing, its fur blending almost perfectly with the icy landscape.

Jake's muscles tensed. He'd dealt with dangerous animals before, but here, in the middle of this unforgiving wilderness, any misstep could be fatal.

"Folks, it looks like our survivalist Jake has just encountered his first real threat—a polar bear!" The announcer's voice rang out, filled with excitement. "Now, for those tuning in, Jake is no stranger to dangerous encounters, but how will he handle this one? And what about Harper? She's got the tent, but will she share it or leave the others to freeze? Stay tuned!"

The broadcast cut to scenes of viewers in their homes, some cheering for the contestants, others debating who would survive the longest. Bets were already being placed, and the tension was palpable. The camera zoomed in on Jake, his expression steely, as the polar bear moved closer.

Harper hadn't noticed the polar bear, but she could feel something watching her. Every instinct told her to move quickly, to get away from the open ground. She found shelter under an overhang of ice, dropping her pack and tent next to her as she crouched low, scanning the horizon. Her breath came out in sharp bursts, each exhale a puff of white mist in the freezing air.

Just then, she heard it—another growl, closer this time. She turned slowly, her heart racing, only to see a pack of wolves in the distance, their eyes glowing eerily against the backdrop of snow.

Back at the control room, the announcer grinned as the screen split between Jake and Harper, each facing their own deadly encounters.

"Two contestants, two deadly situations! Will Harper use her wits to outsmart those wolves, or will they close in before she can react? And Jake—well, he's got a massive polar bear to deal with. We haven't even reached the first alliance, folks, and things are already heating up in the frozen wasteland."

Across the icy expanse, another figure trudged through the snow—Noah. He had been quiet since waking, his mind still foggy from the memory wipe. The biting cold gnawed at him, and his legs ached from walking. The supplies in his pack were meager, and he knew they wouldn't last long in this environment.

He spotted movement on the horizon—a flash of red. Another survivor? He picked up his pace, pushing through the snow toward the figure. As he drew closer, he realized it was Lila, a woman with a determined look on her face, though her movements were cautious.

Noah hesitated. Should he approach her? Form an alliance? He wasn't sure. He scanned the area, knowing that even in this frozen hellscape, danger was never far away.

The ice beneath his feet creaked ominously, and Noah froze in place. The ice sheet was unstable.

Lila turned toward him, her eyes wide as the sound reached her ears. "Don't move!" she shouted, her voice barely audible over the wind. "The ice..."

A loud crack echoed across the tundra as the ice beneath Noah's feet gave way. He fell, plunging into the freezing water below.

"Wow! Did you see that?" the announcer exclaimed, his voice gleeful. "Noah just took a plunge into the ice-cold depths! That's going to be a tough one to come back from, folks. Will Lila save him, or leave him to freeze? This is *The Hunt*, after all, and trust is hard to come by!"

The broadcast cut to another round of commercials, leaving viewers on the edge of their seats, eager to see if Noah would make it out alive.

Jake watched the polar bear approach, calculating his next move. He could see the hunters lurking in the distance, their presence adding to the tension. They weren't making their move yet, but they were always watching, waiting for the right moment. Jake clenched his fists, his breath steady as he prepared to face the beast head-on.

Meanwhile, Harper carefully set up her tent under the ice overhang, her hands shaking from both the cold and the nerves. She wasn't sure how long she could stay hidden from the wolves, but for now, the tent offered a small reprieve from the bitter cold and the dangerous creatures that prowled the ice.

In the distance, the wolves continued to circle, their eyes glowing in the fading light. Harper knew she couldn't stay hidden forever. Sooner or later, she'd have to face the elements, the animals—and the other survivors.

Chapter 3: Hunters in the Frost

The icy landscape remained as unforgiving as ever. As the sun barely crested over the horizon, the cold seemed to intensify, sinking deeper into bones that were already chilled to the core. Scattered across this frozen expanse, the final survivors were starting to realize just how dangerous this place was—not only from the predators stalking them but from the relentless cold.

Noah struggled to keep his head above the freezing water, the ice-cold shock sending his body into survival mode. His limbs flailed, but they were sluggish, the cold sapping his strength by the second. He reached out, trying to grasp the ice sheet that had crumbled beneath him, but it kept breaking under his weight. Panic clawed at his chest.

Just as his vision began to blur, Lila appeared above him, her face tight with concentration. She threw herself down, gripping the edge of the ice with both hands, and extended a piece of cord she had found in her pack.

"Grab it!" she shouted, her voice cutting through the wind.

Noah reached out, his fingers barely grasping the cord. With all the strength she could muster, Lila pulled him up, dragging his soaked body out of the freezing water and onto solid ice.

For a moment, they both lay there, breathless, the harsh wind whipping around them. Noah's teeth chattered uncontrollably, his body shaking from the cold. He was alive, but without heat, he wouldn't be for long.

The camera zoomed in on the dramatic rescue, cutting to the announcer's excited commentary.

"What a close call, folks! Noah just took a dive into the icy depths, but Lila, with some quick thinking and a bit of cord, pulled him back to safety. That's what we like to see—survival instincts kicking in! But the real question is: Can Noah recover from this, or will the cold finish what the ice started?"

THE HUNT: INTO THE FROST 13

Back at home, viewers were glued to their screens, captivated by the near-death experience and already debating whether Noah would make it to the end.

Elsewhere in the frozen wilderness, two more survivors trudged through the snow, each of them alone and trying to make sense of their situation.

Mila, a former wilderness guide, had been relying on her instincts since the moment she woke up. Her background in survival was second to none, and she moved with a sense of purpose, scanning her surroundings with practiced eyes. She knew the dangers that lurked here—cold-weather animals, unstable ice, and now, what she feared the most: hunters.

She paused, crouching low as she noticed a patch of snow disturbed ahead. A trap. Her instincts told her to move quickly but carefully. Whatever these hunters were planning, she wasn't going to fall for it.

Farther off, Derek, a towering man with a sharp gaze, also moved through the snow, though his approach was more direct. A former soldier, Derek's thoughts were focused and calculated. His body moved efficiently through the snow, but even he could feel the cold biting at him. Every minute out here was a battle against time and the elements.

Derek noticed a glint of metal in the distance—possibly a hidden cache. He approached cautiously, knowing that danger lurked beneath the snow, and if the hunters didn't get him, the freezing cold might.

The first move from the hunters came swiftly and without warning.

One of the hunters, moving silently through the snow, spotted Harper from afar. She was struggling to set up her tent, still too close to the wolves that had circled earlier. The hunter set a trap near her position—a hidden net beneath the snow designed to incapacitate the unwary.

As Harper moved, the snow under her shifted. Before she could react, the net snapped up, entangling her legs and pulling her down into the snow. Panic flashed across her face as she struggled against the trap, but the more she fought, the tighter it held her.

"Looks like Harper's in quite the predicament now!" the announcer's voice rang out over the scene. "Caught in one of the hunters' traps, and she's far too close to those wolves for comfort. Can she get herself out before something else finds her first?"

The audience watched in anticipation as Harper continued to struggle against the trap. But the hunters, lurking nearby, didn't move to finish the job. They were watching, waiting for the cold and the fear to take over.

Back with Noah and Lila, time was running out. Noah's soaked clothes were freezing solid, his body quickly losing the fight against hypothermia. Lila had managed to drag him to a small outcrop of rocks that offered a brief respite from the wind, but without warmth, they wouldn't survive much longer.

Lila frantically searched through their packs, pulling out the emergency heat packs. She broke one open and shoved it into Noah's hands, pressing another against his chest. But it wasn't enough.

"We need to find shelter," she muttered, scanning the area for any sign of a cave, an outcrop, anything that could offer protection. Her eyes fell on a ridge in the distance. It looked like there could be a cave beneath it.

"Stay here," she said, her voice firm, though her own fear was mounting. "I'll find something."

Noah could only nod, his lips blue from the cold.

Jake, still keeping his distance from the polar bear he'd spotted earlier, had been watching the hunters from afar. He had seen them set their traps, and he knew what they were capable of. But what unsettled him the most wasn't the traps—it was the cold.

As he moved through the snow, his breath heavy and visible in the air, he realized that while the hunters were a threat, it was the freezing temperatures that would truly decide who lived and who died. The

THE HUNT: INTO THE FROST

supplies they had weren't enough, and he knew that without finding a hidden cache soon, the cold would take him before the hunters did.

He moved cautiously, keeping an eye on the horizon. The hunters were somewhere close, and he wasn't planning to be their next target.

Back in the broadcast room, the announcer's voice grew more excited. "The hunters are making their first moves! Harper's caught, Noah's barely hanging on, and our survivalist Jake is playing it smart, keeping an eye on those hunters from a distance. But will the cold take them before the hunters do? And where are those hidden caches? It's only a matter of time before someone finds one—or freezes trying."

The camera cut to a scene of Derek approaching the glint of metal in the snow, the first sign of a hidden cache. He reached down, brushing away the snow to reveal a small metal box. Inside were a few extra heat packs, a flare gun, and an MRE.

Chapter 4: Echoes of Memory

THE HUNT: INTO THE FROST 17

The wind howled through the frozen landscape, whipping the snow into a frenzied storm that blotted out everything in its path. The already harsh environment had taken a turn for the worse, and visibility was now nearly nonexistent. Lila struggled to keep her footing as she made her way back toward Noah's makeshift shelter, her mind racing with thoughts of how she would help him survive the freezing cold.

When she arrived at the outcrop where she had left him, her heart sank.

Noah was gone.

There were no signs of a struggle, no footprints leading away—nothing but the swirling snow and the empty space where he had been. She called out his name, her voice barely cutting through the wind, but there was no response. Panic began to rise in her chest. How could he have disappeared so quickly, and without a trace?

Lila stood there for a moment, frozen in place, her mind trying to make sense of it. But there was no time. The storm was growing fiercer, and if she didn't find shelter soon, she would end up just like Noah—lost to the ice and snow.

Back at the broadcast, the announcer's voice cut through the suspenseful scene.

"Looks like we've had our first mysterious disappearance, folks! Noah has vanished without a trace, leaving poor Lila to fend for herself in this brutal storm. But don't worry—there's always more going on behind the scenes. Where did Noah go? And what does it mean for the rest of our contestants?"

The camera then cut away to show Noah being wheeled into a warm hospital room, his body wrapped in blankets, shivering uncontrollably. He had been found and rescued by the show's medical team, but for the other survivors, his absence was still a mystery.

Jake had found temporary shelter in a small crevice between two towering ice formations. The wind still sliced through the cracks, but it was better than being out in the open. He crouched low, trying to shield himself from the worst of the cold, when something strange happened—a flash, quick and disorienting.

A memory.

It was brief, like a snapshot in his mind—he saw himself standing at the top of a mountain, the air cold but not like this. He remembered looking down at a frozen lake far below, his heart pounding from the climb. There had been a feeling of triumph, of victory. But why?

The image faded as quickly as it had come, leaving Jake confused and unsettled. Was it real? Or just a trick of the mind, brought on by the cold and exhaustion?

He shook his head, trying to focus on the present, but the memory lingered, scratching at the edges of his thoughts.

Farther away, Derek moved through the snow with purpose, his steps heavy but steady. The snowstorm was growing worse, and he knew he needed to find shelter soon. As he trudged forward, his mind began to blur, a strange feeling washing over him.

Flashes of his past flickered in front of his eyes—moments he didn't fully understand. He saw himself in a military uniform, standing at attention as a superior officer barked orders. The weight of the gun in his hand, the cold steel, was all too familiar. But he couldn't place the memory exactly. Where was he? Why was he there?

The flashes left him feeling disoriented, and frustration bubbled up in his chest. The memories gave him no answers, only more questions, and in the middle of the storm, they were nothing but a distraction.

Derek grit his teeth, shaking the thoughts from his mind as he pushed forward.

"Looks like the cold isn't the only thing getting to our contestants," the announcer's voice chimed in. "We're seeing the first signs of those memory flashes—glimpses of who they were before *The Hunt*. But will those memories help them survive, or just confuse them even more?"

The audience watched as the storm raged on, each contestant battling their own inner demons as well as the elements.

As the storm intensified, Harper and Mila, both desperate for shelter, stumbled into each other's paths for the first time. They had been moving blindly through the snow, unaware that they were walking toward each other until they practically collided.

Harper's eyes widened as she saw Mila, her first instinct one of suspicion, but the storm had left her too weak to react with hostility. She wasn't sure if Mila was friend or foe, but at that moment, she was just relieved to see another face.

"We need to find shelter," Mila said, her voice barely audible over the wind. "This storm is going to bury us alive if we stay out here."

Harper nodded, too exhausted to argue. The two of them moved quickly, working together despite the tension between them, searching for any form of protection from the storm's fury.

Meanwhile, in the hospital, Noah was submerged in a hot bath, his body trembling as the warmth slowly brought him back from the brink of hypothermia. His mind, however, was a mess of fragmented thoughts and sensations. As the heat began to seep into his bones, flashes of memory broke through the fog in his mind.

He remembered standing in a courtroom, his hands bound in cuffs. The judge's voice was a distant echo, but the weight of guilt—or maybe innocence—hung heavy in the air. The faces of the people in the gallery blurred, but the sensation of being judged, of being sentenced, was clear.

Noah shook his head, trying to clear the memories, but they persisted. Why was he there? What had he done? The answers eluded him, and it left him feeling disoriented.

After the bath, he was moved to a warm hotel room, complete with food and drink. As he sat on the bed, dressed in clean clothes, he felt a mixture of relief and frustration. He had been rescued, spared from the deadly cold, but it also meant that he was no longer part of *The Hunt*. The screen in front of him flickered to life, showing the others still out there, fighting for survival in the frozen wasteland.

Noah was safe now, watching from the sidelines as the game continued without him. But the memories of his time in the ice—of the cold, the fear—would stay with him, even as he remained a spectator.

Chapter 5: Beneath the Ice

The blizzard howled relentlessly, turning the world into a swirling mass of white. Mia and Harper pushed forward, their bodies aching from the cold, the wind biting into their skin. They knew that staying in the open for too long would mean freezing to death, but finding shelter in this storm felt like an impossible task.

Then they saw it—faint but unmistakable in the distance. A tent, barely standing against the icy gusts, its outline barely visible through the flurry of snow. And next to it, a figure.

"It's someone!" Harper shouted, her voice barely carrying over the roar of the storm.

They hurried toward the figure, their steps unsteady in the snow, only to realize the situation was far worse than they thought. Wolves—huge, white-furred predators perfectly adapted to the arctic—were circling the tent, their growls audible even over the wind.

Lila stood by the tent, her body hunched in fear, clutching a half-raised weapon in her trembling hands. The tent had been hastily erected next to an ice wall, but the wolves were closing in, their eyes gleaming with predatory intent.

"We've got to help her!" Mia yelled, pulling Harper along with her.

Together, the two women charged toward the scene, brandishing whatever they could find to scare the wolves off. Harper grabbed a stick from her pack and flung it toward the wolves, while Mia shouted and waved her arms, trying to appear bigger and more threatening.

The wolves hesitated, startled by the sudden appearance of more humans. They snarled but backed off slightly, giving the women a chance to close in. With a final growl, the wolves slunk away into the storm, leaving Lila panting and exhausted next to the sagging tent.

"Thank you," Lila gasped, her voice shaking. "I didn't think they'd leave."

Mia knelt next to the tent, securing it against the wind. "Are you alright?"

Lila nodded, though her face was pale, her hands still trembling. "I'm fine. Just... shaken."

"We need to get out of here," Harper said, eyeing the wolves' retreat. "They could come back, and the storm is getting worse."

"There's an ice cave not far from here," Mia said. "It'll give us better shelter than this tent."

Lila hesitated for a moment, but the storm was too fierce to argue. Together, they packed up what they could, leaving the tent behind for now, and followed Mia to the ice cave she had spotted earlier.

Inside the cave, the wind was muted, the walls of ice offering them some protection from the storm. They moved cautiously, their breaths visible in the cold air as they explored deeper into the cavern. The ground was slick, and every step felt precarious.

"Careful," Mia warned. "This place doesn't feel right."

As they moved further into the cave, Harper's foot caught on something—a tripwire, thin and nearly invisible in the dim light. She froze, her heart pounding in her chest.

"Mia!" she whispered, her voice trembling. "I think I just set off something."

Mia rushed over, eyes scanning the ground. Before she could react, a section of the ice floor gave way, revealing a deep pit lined with jagged spikes of ice. They had narrowly avoided it.

"Stay close," Mia said, her voice tense. "This cave isn't safe."

Lila, still shaken from the encounter with the wolves, nodded silently. She knew better than to argue now. The three of them moved together, cautiously avoiding any more hidden dangers as they found a small alcove where they could rest.

Meanwhile, back in the broadcast room, the announcer's voice echoed through the speakers.

"Well, well, well! Looks like the wolves didn't get their meal after all! Our contestants are working together now, but how long can this alliance last? And will the cave be their salvation—or their downfall?

Place your bets, folks! Things are only getting colder and deadlier from here!"

The camera cut to shots of viewers eagerly placing bets on the outcome, their excitement palpable as they watched the drama unfold.

Huddled together in the alcove, Mia, Harper, and Lila exchanged wary glances. The storm raged outside, and the hidden dangers inside the cave made it clear that they weren't safe, no matter where they went.

"We'll rest here for now," Mia said, her voice steady. "But we have to stay sharp. Something about this cave isn't right."

Lila nodded, still processing everything that had happened. She had been alone for so long, and now she was part of a fragile alliance, one that could shatter at any moment.

The cold seeped into their bones, but for now, they were safe—at least from the storm. What came next was anyone's guess.

Chapter 6: Cold-Blooded

The howl of the wind had subsided, but the growl of danger was far from gone. Mia, Harper, and Lila had been resting uneasily in the cave, but now they had to move. The cold gnawed at them, a constant reminder that the storm outside wasn't their only enemy. And something else lingered—a feeling, a sense of being watched.

Out in the distance, arctic wolves were on the prowl again, their massive forms cutting through the snow with a predator's grace. This time, they were focused on another survivor—Jake, the cold-weather survivalist. His instincts had been screaming at him for hours, urging him to stay alert. But now, with the wolves tracking him, he had no choice but to fight or flee.

His movements were measured, deliberate. He had broken down the tent he found earlier—the one Lila had hastily abandoned—and packed it neatly, slinging it over his shoulder. But every time he moved, the wolves moved with him, their eyes glowing in the fading light.

He crouched low, hiding behind a ridge of snow, trying to remain unseen. The wolves circled him at a distance, pacing, their breath visible in the cold air. But something about their behavior struck him as strange—they weren't attacking. They were just watching.

Then, from the corner of his eye, he saw something worse: a hunter.

The hunter moved silently, almost blending into the icy landscape. Their weapon gleamed dully in the faint light, and their movements were deliberate, predatory. Jake knew in that instant that the wolves weren't his only threat. The hunter was stalking him, waiting for the right moment to strike.

Jake's mind raced. He didn't have much to defend himself with—just the survival gear he had packed and his instincts. The hunter closed in, and the wolves seemed to melt into the background, almost as if they were indifferent to the hunter's presence.

They weren't attacking the hunter. They weren't even acknowledging him.

Were the wolves trained?

THE HUNT: INTO THE FROST

"Looks like Jake's in trouble, folks!" the announcer's voice crackled through the speakers, excitement dripping from every word. "We've got wolves, we've got hunters, and we've got one survivor caught right in the middle! Will his survival instincts be enough to keep him alive?"

Noah sat in his hotel room, watching the events unfold. His body had warmed, but the memory of the cold water still haunted him. The sting of it, the way it had frozen him to his core—it was something he couldn't shake. He felt better physically, but a part of him still felt abandoned, left to die in the cold.

He watched as the hunter stalked Jake, tension knotting in his chest. He had been there once—on the edge of survival, fighting for his life. Now, he could only sit back and watch, powerless to help.

Back in the icy wilderness, Jake's heart pounded in his chest as the hunter drew nearer. He knew he had only moments to act. His hands fumbled with the gear he had salvaged from the tent. He found the flint and steel, an idea forming in his mind. He crouched low, striking the flint against the steel, the spark igniting the small amount of tinder he had packed.

A small fire flared to life, and the wolves stopped in their tracks, wary of the flames. The hunter hesitated as well, but only for a moment.

Jake didn't wait. He hurled the burning tinder toward the wolves, not to hurt them, but to create a barrier between himself and the predator closing in. The wolves, startled, backed away, their glowing eyes narrowing in the firelight.

The hunter, however, wasn't so easily deterred. They advanced, weapon raised, ready to strike. But Jake had already moved, using the fire as cover, slipping away into the shadows of the snow-covered terrain.

He ran, his breath coming in ragged bursts, his body numb with cold. He could hear the hunter behind him, but he didn't look back. He had survived this long by staying ahead, by outsmarting his enemies.

The wolves weren't following. They had never been his real enemy.

The camera cut back to the announcer, his grin wide as he addressed the audience. "What a move! Jake's fire saved him from the wolves, but the hunter's still out there! What's next for our survivalist? And what about the others—can they survive the cold-blooded predators lurking in the shadows?"

Hours had passed since the polar bear had appeared earlier in the game. For a while, the audience had been left wondering what had happened to the contestant who had encountered the beast. The tension built as the camera panned to where the polar bear had been stalking the figure earlier.

The man—Derek—had managed to escape, but just barely. He had used the terrain to his advantage, climbing higher onto an ice ridge where the bear had difficulty reaching him. He had sustained a few scratches, but he was alive. For now.

Derek crouched low, his body pressed against the ice, as he watched the bear lumber away, disinterested now that the hunt had failed. His heart still raced, adrenaline pumping through his veins. He had survived a polar bear attack, but now he had to survive the cold and the endless white landscape ahead.

Back in the hotel room, Noah sighed, sinking back into the chair. He watched the screen as Jake narrowly escaped the hunter's trap, and Derek continued his journey. The sense of abandonment gnawed at him, even though he knew Lila had done what she had to do. She couldn't have saved him from the cold.

But that didn't change the fact that, in the end, he had been left to freeze.

Chapter 7: Frozen Tears

The cold was biting, but the tension between the survivors was even sharper. Slowly, the scattered group began to find each other, drawn together by necessity. Mia and Harper had been moving cautiously, using the ice cave as temporary shelter, but now they spotted movement in the distance—other survivors.

Jake approached first, his posture tense but calm. He had survived longer than most because of his instincts, but now, with others around, the stakes were different.

"Stay sharp," he muttered as he approached the group, eyes scanning the horizon. "The cold isn't your only enemy out here."

Mia glanced at him, unsure whether to trust this stranger. "What do you mean?"

Jake paused, crouching down to examine the snow. "Wolves," he said quietly, his voice low but firm. "They've been following us. But something's off. They're ignoring the hunters. It's like they've been trained."

Harper frowned, her breath puffing in the cold air. "Trained? What does that mean?"

"I don't know yet," Jake admitted, standing and adjusting the pack he carried. "But it raises questions. Either way, don't let your guard down."

"Looks like the group is finally coming together!" the announcer's voice echoed through the broadcast room, excitement clear in his tone. "But with distrust running high and the wolves still out there, it's anyone's guess who'll survive the longest! Will Jake's survival instincts be enough to save them all, or will betrayal get the better of them first?"

The camera zoomed in on the group as they gathered cautiously, every movement scrutinized by viewers at home. Noah sat forward in his chair, watching closely. Though he was physically warm now, the sting of the cold from the icy water still clung to him. His heart ached slightly as Lila came into view on the screen, and he couldn't shake the feeling of abandonment, despite knowing she had no choice but to leave him.

Still, Noah couldn't help but feel a pang of sympathy. Lila's face showed signs of guilt, her expression weighed down by something far deeper than the cold.

Lila's hands shook as she unpacked what little supplies she had left. The guilt gnawed at her, a constant reminder of her failure. She had left Noah behind. Even though she knew there was nothing more she could've done, it didn't make it easier. His face—pale and cold—flashed in her mind, haunting her every time she closed her eyes.

Mia watched her from a distance, sensing the unease but saying nothing. The cold had a way of amplifying emotions, making guilt and fear even harder to shake off.

As the group huddled together, Jake's knowledge of the environment became invaluable. He took control of the situation almost naturally, giving the others survival tips without thinking twice.

"Don't keep your heat packs too close to your skin," he instructed Harper. "It'll cause burns. You want them layered between your clothes. Keeps you warm without causing damage."

Harper nodded, adjusting the packs as Jake had suggested. It was small advice, but every bit of warmth mattered in this frozen wasteland.

"There's not much food left in these packs," Mia murmured, shaking one of the MREs. "We need to find more supplies."

Jake's face darkened slightly. "I found a cache earlier," he admitted. "But it's gone now. Someone cleared it out."

The group exchanged uneasy glances. The cold was hard enough to survive, but now betrayal? It made everything worse.

Back in the broadcast room, the announcer's voice dripped with suspense. "Uh-oh! Looks like someone's been hoarding supplies. In this frozen wasteland, that's a dangerous game to play. With trust running thin, it's only a matter of time before things get heated!"

The audience at home was glued to the screens, placing their bets on who would crack first.

Lila couldn't shake her guilt, her mind swirling with memories of Noah. She kept glancing around nervously, as if expecting him to appear. When Jake mentioned the wolves again, she stiffened.

"They ignored the hunters?" she asked, her voice filled with disbelief.

Jake nodded. "They were definitely following me, but they paid no attention to the hunters."

"That doesn't make any sense," Harper added. "Why would they be trained?"

"Because we're not the only targets," Jake said, a cold realization settling in his voice. "This isn't just survival. It's something else. And the more I see, the more I think we're not the only ones being watched."

Mia frowned, feeling the unease in his words. "What do you mean?"

Jake paused, scanning the horizon. "I don't know yet. But we need to be prepared for anything."

Lila remained silent, the guilt of leaving Noah and the new revelations about the wolves weighing heavily on her. Trust was hard to come by now, and though they had found each other, the frozen wasteland was doing its best to pull them apart.

Chapter 8: The Ice Floe Gamble

The sun had been up for nearly 24 hours, casting a harsh light over the endless expanse of ice and snow. Jake squinted at the horizon, taking note of the low, unrelenting brightness. His instincts told him they were in one of the polar circles—likely Antarctica, near the South Pole. The endless daylight was a sign, but it was the stars that confirmed it. As the sun finally began to dip, a faint glow of the aurora borealis started to shimmer above them, and Jake knew that they were in for 24 hours of darkness. The temperature was going to drop, and it was going to drop fast.

"We've got maybe an hour before night hits," Jake said to the group, his voice steady but urgent. "Once it does, the temperature's going to plummet. We need to keep moving."

The others nodded, their faces pale from the cold and exhaustion. The terrain ahead was treacherous—a vast ice floe stretching out before them, cracked and unstable. Every step felt like a gamble, with freezing water just below the surface, ready to drag them under if they misstepped.

Harper shivered beside him, rubbing her hands together to keep them warm. "Are we really going to cross this?"

Jake didn't hesitate. "We don't have a choice."

As they leaped from one unstable sheet of ice to another, the sound of cracking ice echoed in their ears. The freezing water beneath the surface sloshed ominously, reminding them just how close they were to a deadly plunge. The cold air was biting, but the real danger lay in the unpredictability of the ice beneath their feet.

Mia was the first to notice the shapes in the distance—hunters, moving swiftly along the ice, setting up ambushes. She pointed, her voice low. "They're closing in on us."

Jake's jaw tightened. "Stay low. Move fast. We need to get off this floe before they trap us."

They moved as quickly as they could, but with every leap, the ice threatened to give way. Mia slipped once, her foot plunging into the freezing water, but Harper was there to pull her back up. The cold seeped into her bones, but she pushed on, the sight of the hunters driving her forward.

But not everyone was as lucky.

Lila, struggling to keep up with the group, fell behind. Her body was weak, her mind distracted by the guilt of leaving Noah behind. Her steps faltered, and before she knew it, the wolves were upon her again—silent, swift, their eyes gleaming in the twilight.

She tried to scream, but a dart hit her neck before she could call for help. Her vision blurred as the wolves circled her, and the last thing she saw before blacking out was the rest of the group disappearing into the distance.

When Lila came to, she wasn't on the ice anymore. Instead, she found herself in a warm, comfortable room—safe, but disoriented. As her eyes adjusted to the dim light, she realized she wasn't alone.

"Noah?" she whispered, her voice cracking.

He was sitting in a chair by the window, looking out at the snowstorm raging outside. He didn't turn to face her, but his voice was cold. "You left me."

Lila's heart sank. She had known this moment would come, but it didn't make it any easier. "I didn't have a choice," she said softly. "You know that."

Noah remained silent, his hands clenched into fists. The sting of the cold water still haunted him, and even though he was safe now, the memory of being abandoned cut deeper than the freezing ice.

Back on the ice floe, the rest of the group pressed on, unaware of what had happened to Lila. As night began to fall, the aurora above them cast an eerie glow over the landscape, making everything seem even more surreal.

Jake spotted something up ahead—a cache. He motioned for the others to follow, his breath coming in short, cold bursts. When they reached it, they found a bow and arrows, flares, and a few supplies. It wasn't much, but it was enough to give them hope.

"We can hunt now," Jake said, inspecting the bow. "If we find anything out here."

They didn't have to wait long. Jake's sharp eyes spotted movement in the distance—rabbits, darting across the snow. With quick precision, he strung the bow and released the arrow, hitting his mark.

Within minutes, Jake had killed a few rabbits and was preparing them for cooking. The smell of roasting meat was a small comfort in the frozen wasteland, and the group huddled around the fire, grateful for the warmth and food.

As they ate, it became clear to everyone that Jake's instincts were invaluable. He had kept them alive, guided them through the worst of the terrain, and now he was feeding them.

"We should follow his lead," Mia said quietly, glancing at the others. "He knows what he's doing."

Harper nodded in agreement. "He's right. We need someone to make decisions. Someone who can keep us alive."

Jake, modest as always, shook his head. "I'm just doing what needs to be done."

But it was clear—he had proven his value and worth. By the end of the night, the group had voted him their leader, trusting him to guide them through the freezing hell they found themselves in.

As the fire crackled and the stars above shimmered, Jake couldn't shake the feeling that something was still wrong. The wolves, the hunters, the trained animals—it all felt like pieces of a puzzle he couldn't quite put together.

And as the temperature dropped further and the darkness deepened, the real danger was only just beginning.

"And there you have it, folks!" the announcer's voice crackled with excitement. "A daring escape across the ice, a brutal showdown with the elements, and our man Jake stepping up as the leader of the pack. But what about Lila? Dragged off by wolves, hit by a dart, and now reunited with Noah. The game's heating up, even as the temperature drops! Stay tuned, because things are about to get even colder—and deadlier—in *The Hunt*!"

Chapter 9: Frozen Prey

THE HUNT: INTO THE FROST

The cold air bit at Mia's skin as she carefully navigated the narrow ice shelf. Her breath came in sharp bursts, disappearing into the freezing mist swirling around her. The ice beneath her feet cracked ominously, reminding her with every step that one wrong move could send her plummeting into the icy waters below.

But it wasn't just the ice she had to worry about—the hunter had finally caught up to her.

Standing at the edge of the shelf, the hunter loomed like a shadow, weapon in hand, watching her with a predator's intensity. Instead of rushing in, they seemed to enjoy the game, taking their time, herding her toward a trap. Every step Mia took backward edged her closer to danger.

"You're cornered," the hunter called out, their voice low and mocking. "Nowhere to run."

Mia's mind raced, and her heart pounded in her chest. The ice beneath her creaked again, the sound reverberating through her bones. But as panic bubbled inside her, a spark of instinct flickered—a survival strategy she hadn't realized she remembered. The ice, treacherous as it was, could be used to her advantage.

The hunter stepped closer, clearly relishing the chase. But Mia made her move. Instead of retreating further, she shifted her weight and stomped hard on a fragile patch of ice.

The sharp crack echoed loudly as the ice splintered beneath them. The hunter froze, eyes widening in realization, but it was too late. The ground gave way, sending the hunter tumbling into the dark void below. Mia didn't look back as the hunter vanished into the icy depths.

Standing at the edge, Mia breathed heavily, staring into the dark ice cave below. The hunter was gone, but was it permanent? The freezing cavern swallowed the hunter's fate in mystery.

With no time to dwell on it, Mia turned and continued across the ice, the cold stinging her face, her narrow escape leaving her shaken but alive.

"Well, folks, how's that for a turn of events?" the announcer's voice rang out, filled with excitement. "Mia outsmarts her hunter and sends them crashing into the ice cave below! But don't count that hunter out just yet. They might just come back for round two. Keep those bets rolling in!"

The camera cut to shots of viewers furiously placing bets, eagerly debating whether the hunter was gone for good or if they would make a comeback. The stakes had never been higher, and everyone was on edge.

Back in the warmth of the hotel room, Noah sat beside Lila, the tension between them starting to ease. The events of the game played out on the screen before them, but it was their own unspoken conflict that held the weight.

"I've been thinking," Noah said, breaking the silence. His voice was softer than before. "If I'd been in your place... I might've done the same thing."

Lila looked at him, her guilt clear in her eyes. "I didn't want to leave you, Noah. But I... I had to."

"I know," Noah replied, the sting of being left behind still lingering, but less raw now. "We both did what we had to do to survive."

For the first time since their reunion, they shared a look of understanding. The tension between them melted just a little, though they both knew that trust—especially in this world—was fragile and easily broken.

Chapter 10: Shattered Ice, Shattered Trust

••••

ite Jake's hunting skills and his ability to navigate the frozen wasteland, their food supplies were dwindling rapidly. The cold was worsening, biting through even their thickest layers of clothing, and the endless expanse of snow stretched before them like a bitter promise of survival against impossible odds.

Jake had managed to catch a few rabbits, but it wasn't enough. The meager portions they had were barely sustaining them, and the relentless cold was draining their energy faster than they could replenish it. Mia, Harper, and the others were on edge, their nerves frayed from the hunger and the harsh environment.

"We're not going to make it if we keep going like this," Harper muttered under her breath, glancing suspiciously at Mia. "Someone's been eating more than their share."

Mia scowled, exhausted but unwilling to let the accusation pass. "Are you serious right now? We've been splitting everything evenly."

"That's not what it looks like," Harper shot back, her voice rising in frustration. "We barely have anything left, and someone's taking more than they should."

Jake, sensing the growing tension, tried to step in. "We're all in this together. We need to stick to the plan."

But it was no use. The cold, the hunger, and the desperation were too much. The bonds they had formed were beginning to break, and suspicion gnawed at them like the icy wind.

"Looks like our survivors are starting to turn on each other," the announcer's voice echoed through the broadcast. "Tensions are high, supplies are low, and with the cold worsening, it's only a matter of time before someone snaps. Who's going to make it through? And who's going to fall victim to the ice?"

As the group trudged across another stretch of frozen terrain, their steps became heavier, more labored. Every breath they took sent icy tendrils through their lungs, and the silence between them was thick with distrust.

Then, without warning, the ice beneath Harper's feet gave way.

A sharp crack echoed through the air as the ground disappeared from beneath her, sending her plunging into the freezing water below. The shock of the cold hit her like a sledgehammer, stealing the breath from her lungs and freezing her limbs almost instantly.

"Harper!" Mia screamed, rushing to the edge of the hole, but the others hesitated, unsure whether to help or save themselves.

Harper's hands flailed as she tried to grasp onto the jagged edges of the ice, but the freezing water pulled her down, sapping her strength with every passing second. The cold was unbearable, her body going numb as she struggled to stay above the surface. Her breath came in ragged gasps, her heart racing in her chest.

The others stood by, helpless, as Harper's head slipped beneath the icy water.

The warmth seeped into her bones, and for a moment, she forgot where she was. Her mind was foggy, the memories of the ice and the freezing water already beginning to fade.

But as she sat up in the bath, reality came flooding back. The ice, the water... she had fallen through.

She looked around, confused, as her surroundings came into focus. She was in a hotel room, a fire crackling in the fireplace. The room was cozy and warm, the complete opposite of the frozen wasteland she had been in just moments before. A large TV screen was mounted on the wall, playing the events of *The Hunt*, her fellow survivors still battling the cold and each other.

But Harper wasn't alone.

Noah sat in a chair by the fire, his eyes flickering between the screen and Harper. Next to him, Lila sat quietly, her gaze distant. They both looked up as Harper wrapped herself in a towel and stepped out of the bath, still disoriented by the sudden change. There was food on the table—warm and plentiful—but Harper barely noticed as she took in her surroundings.

Noah offered her a nod, his expression one of understanding. "Welcome to the other side," he said quietly, his voice tinged with the memory of his own experience.

Lila glanced at Harper, a mixture of guilt and relief in her eyes. "It's... strange, isn't it?" she said softly.

Harper stared at the screen, watching the others fight to survive. Her time in *The Hunt* was over, but she couldn't shake the feeling that something still wasn't right.

"And just like that, Harper's out of the game!" the announcer's voice rang out triumphantly. "But don't worry, folks—she's safe and warm now, enjoying the comforts of our recovery room while the others continue to fight it out in the freezing cold. Keep those bets coming in, because things are only going to get more intense from here!"

Chapter 11: Memories Thaw

THE HUNT: INTO THE FROST

The cold gnawed relentlessly at the survivors, but now it wasn't just the elements they were battling. Flashes of memory broke through their minds—disjointed, fractured pieces of their pasts that added confusion to their already dire situation. The drug that had wiped their memories was wearing off, but it wasn't quick. It teased them with fragments, leaving them guessing and disoriented.

Jake led the group through the ice, his survival instincts sharper than ever. But those instincts weren't the only thing kicking in. Small flashes—brief moments of clarity—interrupted his focus. He saw a contract, faces from his past, moments that felt both familiar and distant. Yet, nothing was clear. His suspicions were growing, but he couldn't put the pieces together yet.

Mia trudged behind him, her face pale and her body trembling. "I keep seeing things," she muttered, more to herself than to anyone else. "Why can't I remember anything clearly?"

Jake glanced back but didn't stop moving. "The drug... it's wearing off, but slowly. We'll remember, eventually."

"But what if it's too late by then?" Mia asked, her voice filled with worry.

Jake didn't answer. He was too focused on their surroundings, on staying alive. But even as he pushed forward, the flashes of memory continued. They were starting to add up—pieces of a puzzle that wasn't yet fully formed.

In the warmth of the hotel room, Harper, Noah, and Lila sat watching the broadcast on the large screen, but unlike before, their minds were no longer clouded by confusion. The moment they had been rescued, they had been given an injection—a swift shot that restored their memories in full. The flood of information had hit them like a tidal wave, and now they sat there, fully aware of who they were and why they had volunteered for the game.

Harper leaned back in her chair, her mind replaying the events that had led her here. She had agreed to be part of *The Hunt*, but the memory of that decision had been wiped clean until now. The reasons were still fresh in her mind—desperation, money, a way out. But now, knowing the truth, she wasn't sure if she could stomach watching the others struggle.

"I can't believe we agreed to this," Harper said, shaking her head as she watched Mia and Jake trudge through the snow.

"They'll remember soon enough," Lila replied, her tone resigned. "The drug wears off after a few days, and they'll get their memories back. But by then... it might be too late."

Noah, sitting silently in the corner, stared at the screen. His own memories had come flooding back the moment he was taken out of the game. He remembered every detail now—the paperwork, the promises, the risks. It had all seemed so straightforward back then, but watching it play out was a different kind of horror.

"They'll survive," Noah finally said, though his voice lacked conviction. "Jake's smart. He'll figure it out."

Lila glanced at him, her expression unreadable. "Figuring it out won't save them if the hunters get there first."

"And there you have it, folks!" the announcer's voice boomed through the broadcast. "Our survivors are starting to piece together their pasts, but will those flashes of memory help them or just slow them down? With the hunters closing in and the cold wearing them thin, this game is heating up! And for those already rescued—well, they've got their memories back, but what does that mean for the rest still in the hunt? Keep those bets coming in!"

The camera zoomed in on Jake, his face tense as he scanned the icy horizon.

Jake's suspicions were growing. The flashes of memory weren't making sense, but something was definitely wrong. The way the hunters moved, the way the wolves had acted... it all felt orchestrated, planned. He couldn't shake the feeling that they were being watched, controlled.

"We need to find shelter," Jake muttered, pushing his thoughts aside. Survival came first.

Mia stumbled again, catching herself before she fell. "Jake... I keep seeing things. I think... I think we signed up for this."

Jake's jaw tightened. "I know."

"You remember?" Mia's voice trembled.

"Not yet. Just flashes. But I can tell."

They were on the edge of a larger revelation, but time was running out. The memories were coming back, but they didn't have the luxury of waiting for the full picture. The hunters were closing in, and survival was the only thing that mattered now.

But in the back of his mind, Jake knew the truth would hit them soon. And when it did, they would have to face not just the hunters, but the choices they had made to get here.

Inside the hotel, Noah, Lila, and Harper watched in silence, their memories fully intact now. The injection had given them everything back—the knowledge of the game, their reasons for participating, and the reality of what was at stake.

"They'll figure it out soon," Noah said quietly. "And when they do... they'll understand why we're here."

Lila didn't respond. She just kept watching the screen, knowing that the game wasn't over yet. Not by a long shot.

Chapter 12: Blizzard of Betrayal

THE HUNT: INTO THE FROST

The wind howled, its icy fingers clawing at the remaining survivors as they struggled to find shelter. The blizzard had come without warning, a wall of white fury that erased the landscape, making every step treacherous. Visibility was near zero, and the cold bit into their skin like knives, cutting through even their thickest layers of clothing. The storm wasn't just a physical threat—it was the perfect cover for hidden dangers lurking in the snow.

Jake led the way, his instincts guiding him through the storm. It had been days since they'd had a proper meal, surviving on the last scraps of their rations. Hunger gnawed at their stomachs, weakening them further in the face of the cold. But luck seemed to turn when Jake spotted movement in the distance. An Arctic fox, sleek and white, darted through the snow, unaware of the starving humans nearby.

Without hesitation, Jake raised his makeshift spear and threw it with precision honed by years of survival training. The spear found its mark, striking the fox cleanly. The others gathered around as Jake retrieved the kill, relief flooding through them. They would have something to eat, even if only for a short while.

"Get a fire going," Jake ordered as he began preparing the fox for cooking. His hands worked quickly, despite the biting cold.

Mia, shivering, helped gather what little dry wood they could find. The group huddled around the small fire, grateful for the warmth as the scent of cooking meat filled the air. But something was wrong. The rations they had left, meager as they were, had disappeared.

Mia's eyes widened as she scanned the group. "Where's the rest of the food?"

Jake's gaze hardened, and he turned toward the others. "Someone's been hiding it."

The fire crackled as they all stood there, the tension rising in the small shelter. It didn't take long for Jake to notice Kyra's guilty expression. She tried to avoid his gaze, but Jake's eyes narrowed.

"Kyra," Jake said, his voice low and dangerous. "What did you do?"

Kyra backed away, clutching her coat. "I—I was just trying to survive! I thought if I took a little extra... I didn't mean to—"

"You've been hoarding supplies while the rest of us starved?" Mia's voice was sharp with anger. "We've barely made it through this, and you've been keeping food from us?"

Kyra's face twisted in panic. "I didn't think it would hurt anyone! I just—"

Jake stepped forward, cutting her off. "You know what hoarding does out here. You've been putting us all in danger. This storm could kill us, and you made sure we were too weak to survive."

Kyra's eyes darted around, searching for a way out, but there was none. The group's trust had been shattered. Without another word, Jake motioned toward the entrance of the shelter. "Get out."

Kyra's expression turned to disbelief. "What? You can't just throw me out there! I'll die!"

"You should have thought about that before you betrayed us," Jake said coldly. The others, though hesitant, nodded in agreement. Trust was a fragile thing in this environment, and Kyra had broken it beyond repair.

With no other options, Kyra stumbled out into the storm, the blizzard swallowing her form within seconds. But Jake knew the storm wasn't the only threat. The hunters had been watching, waiting for any sign of weakness. And Kyra, cast out into the white fury, was easy prey.

It didn't take long for the hunters to find her. The sound of their boots crunching through the snow was the only warning she got before they descended upon her. Kyra's screams were brief, cut off by the howling wind as the hunters made quick work of their target. She had been too weak, too desperate to put up a fight.

Her body disappeared into the storm.

Kyra jolted awake, her body still shaking from the cold. She looked around, disoriented, before realizing where she was. The hotel room was warm, with a fire crackling in the fireplace, and the scent of food filled the air. She had been pulled from the game—rescued, but at a price. Her betrayal had cost her everything.

Across the room, Noah, Harper, and Lila sat watching her. They said nothing, but their expressions said enough. She had become just another contestant who had been taken out, her memories restored by the injection, leaving her to grapple with the weight of her actions.

The large screen in front of them flickered to life, showing Jake and the others still huddled in the shelter, their figures barely visible through the blizzard.

"Well, well, folks!" the announcer's voice boomed through the broadcast. "Looks like Kyra's betrayal didn't pay off! She thought hoarding supplies would keep her safe, but out here in *The Hunt*, betrayal doesn't go unpunished. Now, with the hunters closing in and the blizzard raging, our remaining contestants are facing even tougher odds! What a shocking twist for our audience!"

The camera zoomed in on Jake's group, their faces etched with exhaustion and anger. The audience was buzzing with excitement as the drama continued to unfold, the host's grin widening with each turn of events.

Back in the shelter, the group sat in silence, eating the small portions of the Arctic fox. The betrayal had shaken them all, but there was no time to dwell on it. The hunters were still out there, and the storm wasn't letting up. If they didn't keep moving, Kyra wouldn't be the only one to fall.

Jake stared out into the blizzard, his mind racing. The game was changing, and the stakes were higher than ever.

Chapter 13: The Hunter Becomes the Hunted

THE HUNT: INTO THE FROST

The cold had become an almost constant companion to Jake and Mia as they pressed forward through the endless expanse of snow. Their bodies ached from days of hunger and exhaustion, but the fire inside them still burned. The hunters were getting closer—too close for comfort. But Jake had a plan, and for the first time since the game had started, they weren't just surviving. They were preparing to fight back.

"We can't keep running," Jake said, his voice low as he crouched beside Mia, hidden behind a ridge of ice. "The hunters have the advantage in this storm. They know this terrain better than we do."

Mia shivered, her face pale from the cold. "So what do we do?"

Jake glanced around, scanning the environment for anything they could use to their advantage. "We turn the tables. We set a trap."

Mia's eyes widened. "A trap? How?"

Jake's survival instincts were kicking in. The snow, the ice, the freezing temperatures—they weren't just obstacles; they could be used as tools. He quickly explained his plan to Mia, and despite her exhaustion, a glimmer of hope sparked in her eyes. They weren't just prey anymore.

Using what little gear they had, along with scavenged materials from the environment, Jake and Mia set to work. The blizzard still raged, making visibility difficult, but that was exactly what they needed. The hunters, too confident in their advantage, wouldn't see what was coming.

Hours passed before they heard the sound of footsteps crunching through the snow. Jake and Mia lay still, waiting, their hearts pounding in their chests. The trap was set. Now they just had to wait.

A shadowy figure appeared in the distance—a hunter, moving silently through the storm, their breath fogging up the visor of their mask. Jake's pulse quickened as the hunter drew closer. Any wrong move could mean the end for them.

The hunter stepped into the designated spot, and with a swift motion, Jake triggered the trap. A hidden snare snapped up, entangling the hunter's legs and sending him crashing to the ground.

Mia gasped in surprise as Jake quickly moved in, disarming the hunter before they had a chance to fight back. With the hunter incapacitated, Jake rifled through the man's pack, finding exactly what they needed—heavy cold weather gear, weapons, and rations.

"This is it," Jake whispered to Mia, handing her one of the thick coats. "This will give us a fighting chance."

Mia's hands trembled as she took the gear, her eyes flicking between Jake and the hunter. "What about him?"

Jake paused, his mind racing. They could leave the hunter to freeze to death, or worse, but something inside him resisted that idea. He knew what it was like to be left behind in the cold, and despite everything, he wasn't about to become like the hunters.

"We leave him alive," Jake said firmly. "He's no threat to us now."

Together, Jake and Mia dragged the hunter into a small cave nearby, setting up a small fire to keep him warm. They left behind just enough rations to keep him alive, but not enough for him to follow them quickly.

Mia watched as Jake worked. "Why help him? He would've killed us."

Jake stood, looking down at the unconscious hunter. "Because we're not like them. We're better than them."

Inside the hotel room, Noah, Harper, and Lila sat watching the broadcast, their hearts pounding as they saw Jake and Mia outsmart the hunter. The tension that had gripped them during the trap's setup was finally released, and they couldn't help but cheer.

"They did it!" Harper exclaimed, a smile breaking through her usually serious demeanor. "They actually did it!"

Noah nodded, a rare look of admiration on his face. "That was smart. And leaving the hunter alive... that took guts."

Lila leaned forward, her eyes locked on the screen. "They might just make it."

The announcer's voice crackled through the broadcast, filled with excitement. "Ladies and gentlemen, what a move! Jake and Mia have turned the tables on the hunters, and they've done it with skill and heart! Not only did they outsmart their pursuers, but they showed compassion by leaving the hunter alive! What a twist! The audience is going wild!"

The camera panned to the roaring crowd, who were on the edge of their seats, some cheering for the survivors, while others, disappointed by the hunter's capture, muttered in frustration.

Back in the storm, Jake and Mia, now equipped with heavy cold weather gear and weapons, moved with newfound confidence. The rations they had scavenged would keep them alive for a little longer, but more importantly, they had hope. They could fight back.

"We need to keep moving," Jake said, adjusting his gear. "The others will come looking for him soon."

Mia nodded, her resolve hardened. "We can win this."

Jake gave her a brief smile. "Yeah. We can."

For the first time since the game had started, Jake felt like they had a real chance. The hunters were relentless, but now, so were they. The game had changed. And this time, the survivors weren't just running—they were hunting.

Chapter 14: Frostbite

THE HUNT: INTO THE FROST

The wind had only grown harsher overnight, the freezing air biting into Jake and Mia as they trudged forward through the snow. Their new gear had helped, but it wasn't enough to stave off the relentless cold. The fire they had built the night before flickered weakly, barely enough to keep the worst of the frost at bay.

Mia had grown quieter as the day dragged on. Her steps had slowed, and Jake couldn't help but notice how pale she'd become. Her hands trembled as she tried to adjust her coat, and her lips were turning blue.

"You okay?" Jake asked, though he already knew the answer.

Mia nodded weakly, but she couldn't hide the pain in her face. "It's just the cold. I'll be fine."

But she wasn't fine. The frostbite was setting in, and Jake could see it in the way she moved. Her fingers were stiff, her feet dragging as if they weighed twice as much. He didn't say anything, but he knew she wouldn't last much longer. The cold had taken too much from her.

As the night wore on, Mia's condition worsened. They set up camp in a small alcove of rocks, trying to block the wind as much as possible. The fire crackled feebly, its warmth barely reaching them. Jake watched Mia as she drifted off to sleep, her body trembling even in the thick gear they had scavenged from the hunter.

"I'll keep watch," Jake said quietly, more to himself than to her. He wasn't sure if Mia had even heard him.

Hours passed, and the snowstorm outside raged on. The cold seeped into Jake's bones, but he kept himself moving, checking the fire, listening for any signs of the hunters. He glanced over at Mia several times, hoping she would wake up and reassure him that she could keep going.

But when dawn broke, Mia was gone.

Jake's heart pounded as he scrambled to where she had been lying. Her gear was still there, untouched, but Mia had vanished. He scoured the area, looking for footprints, for any sign of struggle. But the storm had wiped everything clean. It was as if she had simply disappeared into the snow.

Jake stood still, his breath heavy in the freezing air. Had the hunters taken her in the night? Or had the cold finally claimed her? The not knowing gnawed at him, but there was no time to dwell on it. He was alone now, and the clock was ticking.

Inside the hotel, Mia jolted awake in a warm bed, her body still aching from the cold. The fire in the fireplace glowed brightly, and the room felt like paradise compared to the freezing wasteland she had just left. It took a moment for her to remember where she was, but when she did, the weight of the game hit her hard.

She looked over at the screen on the wall, where the game continued. Jake was still out there, alone now. Her heart ached as she watched him scan the snow for her. He didn't know that she had been taken, didn't know that she was safe, recovering.

In the hotel lobby, the tension was palpable. Noah, Harper, and Lila sat in silence, their eyes glued to the screen. The audience, too, was on edge, unsure of what had happened to Mia.

"She's gone," the announcer's voice rang out. "Was it the hunters? The wolves? Or the cold itself? Jake is left alone to face the elements, but the real danger is closing in..."

Back in the frozen wasteland, Jake pushed forward, every step more grueling than the last. The weight of Mia's disappearance hung heavily on him, but he couldn't stop. The cold was merciless, and the hunters were out there—he could feel it. His survival instincts kicked into overdrive, but even those could only carry him so far.

The growl of something large echoed through the storm. Jake's heart raced as he turned to see a familiar silhouette in the distance. The polar bear. It had returned.

And it wasn't alone.

Wolves appeared on the horizon, their yellow eyes glowing through the snow, moving with calculated precision. They circled closer, their breath visible in the frigid air. But it wasn't just the animals. The hunters were closing in too, their dark forms barely visible through the blizzard.

THE HUNT: INTO THE FROST

Jake's hand tightened around the spear he had fashioned, but even he knew the odds were stacked against him. The polar bear growled again, the wolves snarled, and the hunters moved silently into position. Jake was surrounded.

Inside the hotel, Mia watched in horror as the scene unfolded. The screen flickered, showing the wolves, the bear, and the hunters closing in. The tension in the room grew unbearable, the audience barely breathing as they waited to see what would happen next.

"Is this the end for Jake?" the announcer's voice boomed, filled with excitement. "With the cold closing in and predators all around, will he survive this final assault? Stay tuned, folks, as we approach the thrilling conclusion!"

The cold bit into Jake's skin as he stood his ground, the storm howling around him. The polar bear's massive form loomed in the distance, the wolves snarling as they circled. And the hunters, silent and deadly, watched him with unblinking eyes.

Jake's breath came in short, sharp bursts as he prepared for the worst. He had come too far to give up now, but with the odds stacked against him, survival seemed like a distant dream.

The polar bear stepped closer, the wolves closing in, and Jake could feel the hunters' gaze on him. He gripped his weapon tighter, his muscles tense as the storm raged around him.

Chapter 15: The Final Glacier

THE HUNT: INTO THE FROST

The cold winds whipped across the desolate expanse of the glacier, biting at Jake's exposed skin as he trudged forward, every step a battle against exhaustion. The ice beneath his feet cracked and shifted, each step precarious on the unstable surface. His breath came in short bursts, the cold cutting into his lungs as he prepared himself for what felt like the final stand. The polar bear, the wolves, and the hunters were all closing in, and Jake knew there was nowhere left to run.

But as he readied himself to fend off the attack, something strange happened. The bear, massive and imposing, suddenly stopped its advance and sat down on the ice. The wolves, once snarling and circling him, halted and sat as well, their glowing yellow eyes watching him in eerie silence.

Jake blinked, his heart pounding in his chest as he tried to make sense of what was happening. His grip tightened around his makeshift spear, but no attack came. The cold wind howled around them, but the predators remained still, as if waiting for something.

And then, from the whiteout of the blizzard, one of the hunters emerged. His dark silhouette moved slowly, deliberately, and as he drew closer, Jake realized the hunter was walking toward him with no weapon drawn. Jake's mind raced, every instinct telling him to remain on guard, but something about the hunter's approach felt different.

The hunter stopped a few feet in front of Jake, raising one hand in a gesture that signaled peace. Slowly, deliberately, he reached up and removed his mask, revealing a face that Jake didn't recognize—but there was something familiar in the hunter's eyes.

"Jake!" the hunter called out, his voice barely audible over the wind. "It's over. You've done it."

Jake stared at the man, unsure of what to say. His body was tense, ready for a fight that suddenly seemed unnecessary.

The hunter pointed behind Jake, and that's when he heard it—the unmistakable sound of a helicopter's rotors slicing through the air. Jake turned, his heart racing as the blizzard parted just enough for him to see the massive aircraft landing nearby, the wind from the blades kicking up snow in every direction.

Before Jake could react, a heavy fur coat was thrown across his shoulders. The warmth was immediate, almost overwhelming after days of exposure to the freezing cold. The hunter stepped closer, his expression softening.

"Get in," the man said, nodding toward the helicopter. "It's over. You've won."

Jake hesitated for a moment, still trying to process everything, but his body was too weak to argue. He allowed himself to be guided toward the waiting helicopter, his steps heavy and unsteady as the cold finally began to catch up with him.

The warmth inside the helicopter hit him like a wave, enveloping him in a comforting embrace. Jake slumped into one of the seats, the fur coat wrapped tightly around him. The hunter climbed in after him, closing the door as the helicopter lifted off into the storm.

The world outside became a blur of white and gray as the helicopter ascended, leaving the glacier and the icy wilderness behind. Jake leaned back in the seat, his mind spinning. He felt a sharp prick against his neck and turned to see the hunter pressing a hypo-spray against his skin.

"You'll start remembering everything soon," the hunter said calmly. "Just relax."

Jake barely had time to register the words before the drug started to take effect. His memories, once fragmented and distant, came flooding back in vivid detail. He remembered everything—signing up for *The Hunt*, the risks, the challenges, the cold reality of what he had agreed to. The weight of it all hit him at once, but there was no time to dwell on it. The helicopter ride was a blur of exhaustion and fading adrenaline.

When they landed, Jake was taken to an infirmary, where doctors checked him over thoroughly. He was too weak to protest, too numb from the cold and the emotional toll of the game to fully grasp what was happening. After the examination, he was led to a warm hotel room, where a fire crackled in the fireplace. The warmth of the room was both a blessing and a shock to his system after the frozen wasteland he had just left behind.

In the room, waiting for him, were the other survivors—Noah, Harper, Lila, Mia, and Erin—now fully recovered and sitting comfortably. They looked at Jake with a mix of relief and admiration. He was the last one. The final survivor.

Before he could say anything, the door opened, and the announcer walked in, followed by several producers. They clapped and cheered as they entered, their faces alight with excitement.

"Jake, congratulations!" the announcer boomed, his voice filled with energy. "You've done it! The final survivor of this season's *Hunt*!"

The producers crowded around, shaking his hand, patting him on the back, and offering their congratulations. Jake, still overwhelmed by the flood of memories and the exhaustion weighing on him, could only nod.

One of the producers stepped forward. "We know it wasn't easy, and we understand there were hardships, but rest assured, you're a hero now. And of course, there's the matter of your reward."

Jake blinked, still processing everything as the producer handed him an envelope. Inside was a check—an amount so substantial that it almost didn't seem real. But it was. He had earned it.

The announcer beamed, glancing around at the group. "And let's not forget—everyone here, guilty or innocent, has earned their freedom. For the criminals, your records have been wiped clean. For the volunteers... well, you're now heroes in the eyes of the public."

Jake looked around at the others, seeing the weight of their experiences in their faces. They had all gone through hell, but they had survived. And now, it was over.

The following week was a whirlwind of interviews with various news programs. Jake and the others found themselves in the spotlight, praised for their courage and endurance. *The Hunt* had captured the public's imagination, and they were now household names.

As Jake sat in yet another interview, answering the same questions he had heard a dozen times before, he couldn't help but think back to the ice, the cold, the moments when survival seemed impossible. It was all over now, but the memories would stay with him forever.

And then, in the midst of all the attention, the announcer's voice echoed in his mind as he teased the next season of *The Hunt*.

"A new environment," the announcer had said with excitement. "Next season... the desert."

Jake's eyes narrowed as he listened to the details. It was over for him, but *The Hunt* would continue. And there would be new survivors—new victims.

Don't miss out!

Visit the website below and you can sign up to receive emails whenever Edward Heath publishes a new book. There's no charge and no obligation.

https://books2read.com/r/B-A-WXZX-DYNAF

BOOKS 2 READ

Connecting independent readers to independent writers.

Did you love *The Hunt: Into the Frost*? Then you should read *In the Shadow of the Hunt*[1] by Edward Heath!

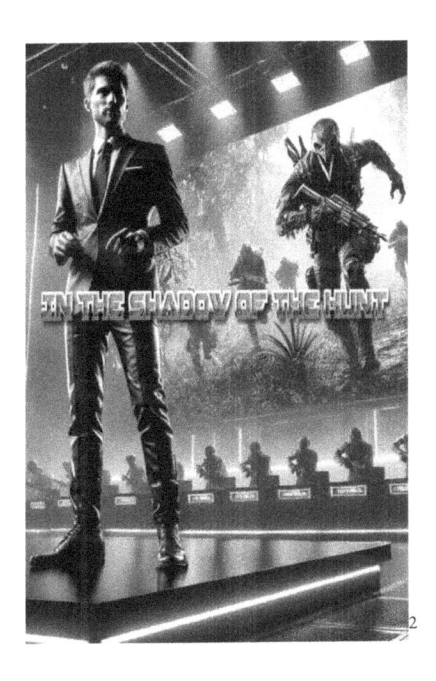

In a not-so-distant future, society's obsession with entertainment takes a deadly turn.

Criminals are offered a terrifying choice: face their sentence or enter The Hunt, a brutal televised competition where survival means freedom. With armed hunters, deadly traps, and a jungle teeming with danger, contestants must outwit their pursuers and each other in a high-stakes battle for their lives—all while the world watches.

Dante, wrongfully convicted and thrust into the chaos, must navigate this savage game while piecing together fragments of his past. As alliances form and betrayals mount, the line between hunter and

---

1. https://books2read.com/u/3yXKGZ

2. https://books2read.com/u/3yXKGZ

hunted blurs. Every moment is a fight for survival, and the only way out is to win.

But in a world where violence is celebrated, and morality is a forgotten relic, how far will one man go to survive?

Prepare for a relentless, action-packed thriller that will keep you on the edge of your seat until the very last page.

Read more at https://twitter.com/Iam8lu3.

About the Author

Edward Heath, a passionate digital artist and book publisher, is committed to an open-minded approach in the arts. My focus is on nurturing diverse talents and bringing unique perspectives.**https://linktr.ee/IamBlu3https://X.com/Iam8lu3**
Read more at https://twitter.com/Iam8lu3.

Milton Keynes UK
Ingram Content Group UK Ltd.
UKHW040808051024
449151UK00001B/51